First published in Great Britain in 1998 by Andersen Press Ltd., 20 Vauxhall Bridge Road, London SW1V 2SA.
Published in Australia by Random House Australia Pty., 20 Alfred Street, Milsons Point, Sydney, NSW 2061.
All rights reserved. Colour separated by Fotoriproduzioni Grafiche, Verona.
Printed and bound in Italy by Grafiche AZ, Verona.

10   9   8   7   6   5   4   3   2   1

British Library Cataloguing in Publication Data available.
ISBN 0 86264 791 6

A Sunday with Grandpa

PHILIPPE DUPASQUIER

Andersen Press • London

in memory of Ron Burgess

Today is Sunday,
and we are on our way to visit my grandpa.

My grandpa is very old.
He lives by himself on a farm in the countryside.

He is coming to meet us at the station
in his funny old car.

"Hello, Grandpa... Isn't it a lovely day for our picnic?"
We all pile into the car.
"Off we go!" says Grandpa.

In the corner of the farmyard
stands the old broken-down tractor.
My brother and I love playing on it.
My turn to be the driver!

Grandpa is very proud of his vegetable garden.
He shows us his rows of runner beans...

and gives us carrots to feed the rabbits.

But I like feeding the birds best.
Grandpa gives us bread for them.

My grandpa is a real handyman.
He keeps all his tools in the big shed. What a clutter!
We like making things, too.

"Come on," calls Mum. "It's time for our picnic."

On the edge of the wood we find a good spot for
our picnic. Mum has packed cold chicken
for Grandpa. It's his favourite.
But I like the crisps best.

After lunch we play football with Grandpa.
But we mustn't make him run too fast
because, after all, he is very old.

Because he's so old, Mum worries about him
all the time. She wants him to come and live
with us. But Grandpa gets upset when she talks
about it. "Don't be silly!" he always says...

"I could never live in a town.
And anyway, who would look after my garden?"
He's right, my grandpa. And who
would feed the rabbits?

*Please!
Don't start that
again ...*

My grandpa has always lived in the countryside.
He knows the names of all the flowers...
and all the trees... and all the birds.

He can even find the deer's secret hiding place!

It starts to rain and we have to rush back to the farmhouse.
"Time for a nice cup of tea," says Dad.

"Go and sit down," Mum says to Grandpa, who always wants to do everything himself.

In his desk, Grandpa keeps all his old
photograph albums. There are photographs of
Mum when she was still living on the farm.

Grandpa makes us laugh...
He tells us stories that happened a long time ago,
when Mum was just a little girl.

What a shame! It's already time to go...

But Grandpa doesn't want us to leave empty-handed.
He gives us lettuces and beans fresh from the garden.

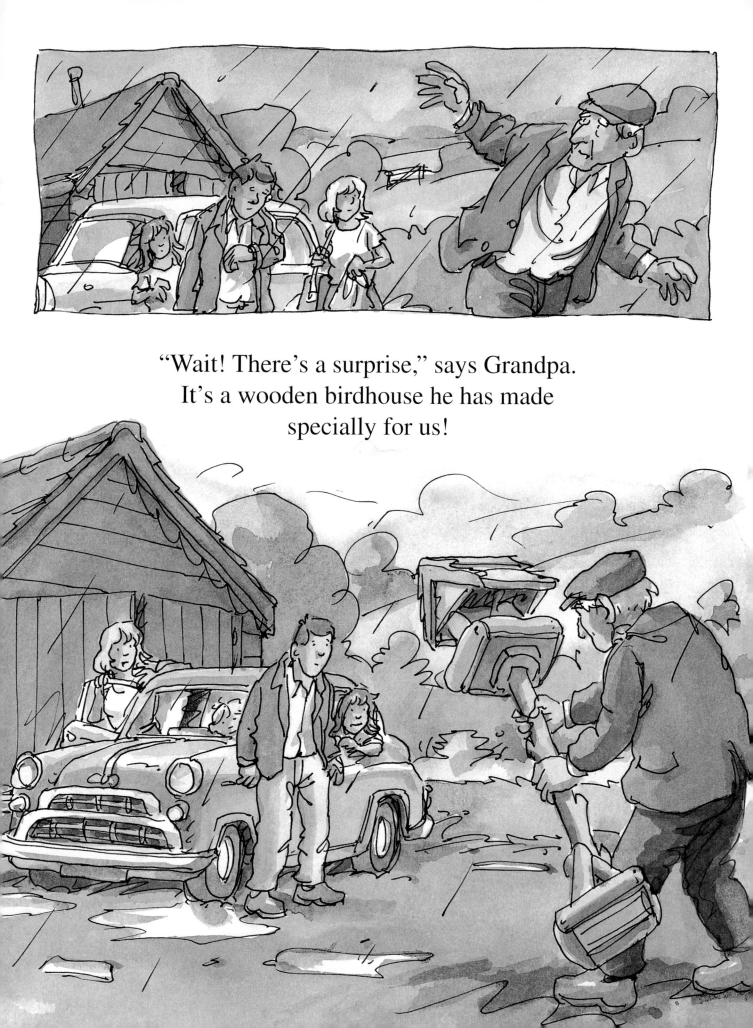

"Wait! There's a surprise," says Grandpa.
It's a wooden birdhouse he has made
specially for us!

"Oh, no! We're going to be late!" Dad keeps saying.
"Don't panic. There's plenty of time," says Grandpa.

"Goodbye, Grandpa. See you very soon.
Thank you for everything."

It's the end of the day and we'll soon be home.
Tomorrow is school again... I think about
the lovely day we've had together.

Grandpa will be back at the farmhouse now.

He must be feeling lonely without us...

With all that rush,
I didn't even have time
to kiss him goodbye.
But I know what I'll do:
I'll write him a letter
and send him a big picture...
That will make him happy.
And it will make me happy, too,
because I love him very much,
my grandpa.

E
DUP

Dupasquier,
Philippe.

A Sunday with
grandpa.

$19.95

YPVE57096

DATE			
Delebrant			
Barenne			
LEB			